# I Want to Be an Athlete and a Teacher

Story by
Garrett Carter

MW00898710

Background story
In the world of children's books, there is underrepresentation of African American characters featured as protagonists. This is why I am here—I want to do my part in chipping away at this void. It is important for children to read stories with characters who are similar to and different than them. Introducing Coby to the world will allow children of color to see themselves and their culture reflected as they read. Additionally, other children will see that someone who does not look like them might still share many of their thoughts, talents, and dreams.

I also firmly believe that children should not limit themselves to one particular dream. What happens if that basketball or football career does not work out? Too many children I speak with have not considered this question seriously. I am not discouraging children from dreaming of becoming the next superstar athlete. I am simply encouraging children to have additional dreams. At the end of each story in "Coby's Athlete and Career Series," Coby realizes that he wants to be an athlete *and* something else, not something else instead of an athlete. Children should not limit themselves by only having one dream; instead, they should have many dreams.

-Garrett

*I Want to Be an Athlete and a Teacher*
Summary: Coby is a young African American boy who is passionate about playing sports. Coby discovers that, in addition to being an athlete, he could make a great teacher!
Text Copyright © 2014 Garrett Carter
Illustrations and Cover Art © 2014 Garrett Carter
Illustrated by Anahit Aleksanyan
Edited by Lisa Beckelhimer

Published in 2014. Printed by CreateSpace. All rights reserved.

ISBN-13: 978-1499152647

Visit the author online: garrettcarterbooks.com and facebook.com/garrettcarterbooks

This book is
dedicated to
our dreamers and
leaders of tomorrow.

Mama, I want to be an athlete when I grow up!

I play sports with my friends and for my school.

I even *dream* about playing sports!

That's great, Coby. I believe in my heart that you can be anything you want to be. But you know … you always want to be prepared to do several things in life.

What do you mean, Mama?

Well, son, you have many gifts and talents. You should explore all of them.

But I don't know what else I could be besides an athlete, Mama. That's what I'm good at.

Oh, Coby, you're good at many other things too! Look at how you helped Lainey yesterday.

Are you talking about her math homework? That was easy!

It might be easy for you, but how did you get *her* to understand math?

Mama, you know how Lainey loves her dolls? Well, I just used her dolls to explain her homework.

I just showed her how if she had eight dolls and then gave away three, then she would have five left.

You knew Lainey would understand if you explained it with her dolls. That was very smart of you, Coby!

It was no big deal, Mama. I sort of enjoyed it -- a little bit.

You enjoyed teaching your sister?

I didn't really think of it as *teaching* her, Mama. I just kind of helped her out.

Like your teacher, Mrs. Shawna, helps you out?

I guess so, Mama. You know, being a teacher might be a fun job. You get to help people understand things in fun ways.

Oh?

Yeah, Mama! There is also recess.

Oh, and I can't forget about grilled cheese and tomato soup lunches!

What's going on in that mind of yours, son?

I think I want to be an athlete *and* a teacher!

Never give up on your dreams, son; just make sure that you always have more than one.

I got an A on my homework last night, Coby! Will you help me again tonight? This time, it's multiplication.

Sure, but we're going to need more dolls.

# The End

What is your game plan?

Name: _____

Age: _____ Grade: _____ Today's Date: _____

What hobbies and activities do you enjoy?

_____        _____

_____        _____

List three jobs you might like to have when you are older and explain why they interest you.

1. _____

Why? _____

_____

2. _____

Why? _____

_____

3. _____

Why? _____

_____

What are you doing now to prepare for your future? _____

_____

To learn more about Coby and "Coby's Athlete and Career Series," visit the author online:

garrettcarterbooks.com

facebook.com/garrettcarterbooks

CPSIA information can be obtained
at www.ICGtesting.com
Printed in the USA
BVHW021723020719
552506BV00007B/64/P